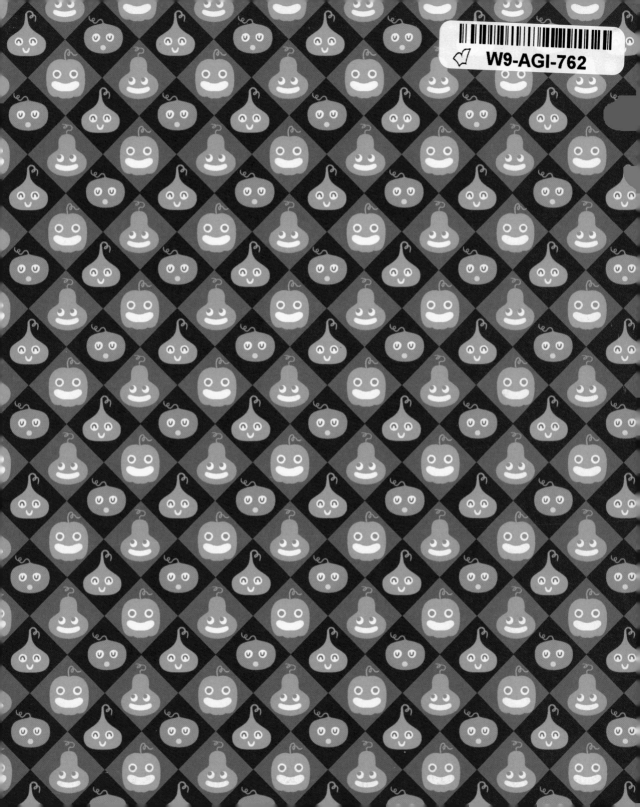

This edition published by Parragon Books Ltd in 2015
and distributed by

Parragon Inc.
440 Park Avenue South, 13th Floor
New York, NY 10016
www.parragon.com

Written by Smriti Prasadam-Halls   Edited by Michael Diggle
Illustrated by Lorena Alvarez   Designed by Vanessa Lovegrove
Production by Charlene Vaughan

ISBN 978-1-4748-0241-3
Printed in China

Pumpkins, Pumpkins Everywhere

Smriti Prasadam-Halls

Lorena Alvarez

PaRragon

Pumpkin happy,

OCTOBER

31

pumpkin sad,

pumpkin kooky,

pumpkin mad.

4th ANNUAL
PUMPKIN PARADE

**HALLOWEEN
BOO-NANZA!**

OCTOBER 31, 7pm

Bring your
carved pumpkins!

Pumpkin bounce,

pumpkin fly,

pumpkin wet

and pumpkin dry.

Pumpkin spider,
pumpkin cat,

pumpkin wolf,
and pumpkin bat!

Pumpkin spooky—
woo! woo! woo!

Pumpkin spooked—
boo hoo hoo!

Pumpkin there,
and there,

and there ...

PUMPKIN PARADE

Pumpkins, pumpkins **everywhere!**

Pumpkin rattle,
pumpkin hoot,

pumpkin jangle,
pumpkin toot.

Pumpkin boogie
to the **beat,**

pumpkin trick and
pumpkin treat.

Pumpkin glowing, pumpkin bright,
shining in the starry night.

Pumpkin brave and not afraid,
lighting up the big parade.

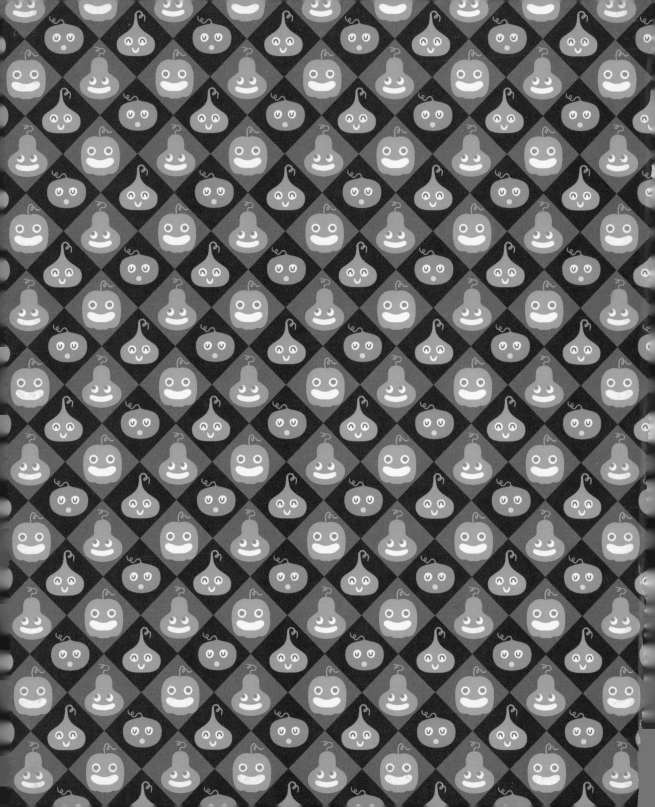